Peter & The Wolf

This book is part of a boxed set
which includes an Enhanced CD
featuring Gavin Friday &
the Friday-Seezer Ensemble
performing Peter & The Wolf.

SERGEI PROKOFIEV'S

Peter & The Wolf

* * *

Illustrated by Bono

WITH JORDAN & EVE

BLOOMSBURY

Peter & The Wolf
Performed by Gavin Friday & The Friday-Seezer Ensemble
Illustrated by Bono with Jordan & Eve

First published in Great Britain 2003

Illustrations © 2003 by Bono
Design © 2003 by Ciarán ÓGaora/Irish Hospice Foundation
Peter & The Wolf , Op.67 by Sergei Prokofiev
© Copyright 1937 by Hawkes & Son (London) Ltd
Reproduced by permission of Boosey & Hawkes Music Publishers Ltd

Music produced and arranged by Gavin Friday and Maurice Seezer

Published by Bloomsbury Publishing, Plc.
38 Soho Square, London W1D 3HB, UK

All papers used by Bloomsbury are natural, recyclable products made from wood grown in
sustainable, well-managed forests. The manufacturing processes conform to the
environmental regulations of the country of origin.

www.peterwolf.org

10 9 8 7 6 5 4 3 2 1

ISBN 0-7475-7060-4

A CIP catalogue record for this book is available from the British Library

Designed by Ciarán ÓGaora
Printed in Hong Kong by Hung Hing Offset

In aid of hospice care

BEWARE ... for wolves come in many disguises.

ONCE UPON A TIME, there was a boy called Peter. He lived with his grandfather in a cottage with a garden surrounded by a high stone wall.

Outside the wall, there was a meadow with a pond and a tall tree. Beyond the meadow was a deep, dark forest.

This is the story of Peter and the wolf.

There's a bird, light and
delicate, with feathers of silk.

A dumb duck with a broad bill
and large, webbed feet.

A pussycat ... She is smooth but greedy and vain.

There is a big grey wolf with
sharp teeth and sharp claws
who is always hungry.

There are hunters, searching the woods, firing their shotguns.

There is a wise old grandfather.

Now, he worries about Peter all the time.

And, of course, there is Peter.

Now, this is where the story begins. Early one morning when Peter walked out of the house, he opened the gate and went into the big green meadow.

On a branch of a tall tree sat a pretty little bird. "All is quiet and beautiful this morning," she said delicately. The bird was Peter's friend. Just then, the dumb duck passed by.

She was glad that the gate had been left open as there was a deep pond in the meadow and she wanted to swim. Seeing the duck, the bird flew down and sat next to her.

The bird, who was very sweet, said:

"*What kind of a bird are you if you can't fly?*"

"*What kind of a bird are you?*" the duck said snappily, "*if you can't swim?*"

And with that, she hurriedly dived into the pond.

That led to an argument.
They argued and argued,
the duck as she splashed
around in the water, the bird
hopping angrily on the shore.

Just then, something caught Peter's eye.
Pussy ... Pussy was stalking through the
tall grass. She thought to herself:
"Hmmm ... That bird is busy arguing. I can
probably get her now."
And on velvet paws, she crept even closer.

"Look out!" shouted Peter, and the bird flew up into the tree just in time.

Well, the duck quacked angrily from the middle of the pond. Pussy walked round and round, looking up at the bird and thinking: "Hmmm ... Is it worth climbing so high, I wonder? By the time I get there she'll have flown away."

BEKED
BEAN
BOY

Grandfather came out of the house and through the open gate. He was puffing on his pipe. He never liked Peter to go out into the meadow.

"Not really the place for you, grandson," he said gravely. "Wolves and things... Do you know anything about wolves, huh? A dangerous lot, those wolves." Peter said nothing. Of course he wasn't afraid of wolves, but then he really couldn't argue with his grandfather. Grandfather led Peter home. He locked the gate securely.

No sooner had Peter gone, than a big grey wolf came out of the dark forest. Pussy turned and saw him. In a twinkle Pussy had scarpered up the tree. And the duck quacked hysterically, but in her panic, foolishly jumped out of the pond.

The wolf saw the duck. He went for her like a shot and no matter how hard, how fast the duck tried to run she could not escape.

The wolf in hot pursuit ... nearer and nearer ... catching up ... catching up ...

Then he got the duck and swallowed her hungrily in one enormous gulp!

Now, this is how things stood. Pussy was up a tree, sitting on one branch, the bird up the same tree on another branch. But not too close to Pussy. There was no great affection between them.

The wolf walked round and round the tree staring at both of them with greedy eyes, licking his lips.

Peter saw it all, thinking: "So the wolf wants to eat them! Well, two can play that game. I'll trap the wolf … yes! That's how it should be done, that's how it must be done!"

So Peter went to his room and found a strong rope, which he wrapped round and round smoothly until he made a noose. He slipped it through his fingers and tried one or two quick throws. He went out, noiselessly climbed up on the stone wall over which one of the branches of the tree stretched. Silently, he took hold of the branch and eased himself on to the tree.

He whispered to the bird:

"Be a good little birdie! Fly down and tease the wolf a bit. Not too close, just enough to keep him busy for a moment or two."

The bird obeyed, fluttering overhead, almost touching the wolf. The wolf leapt upwards, snapping his huge sharp teeth.

But she was a clever little bird and the wolf couldn't catch her!

Meanwhile, Peter took the rope firmly in his hand, and, without the wolf knowing it, he slid the noose over the wolf's tail, ever so gently. Then he pulled the rope with all his might. "*Yes!*" The wolf was caught!

Caught by the tail, the wolf went mental, jumping wildly, trying to escape. Then, Peter tied his end of the rope to the tree. The more the wolf struggled, the tighter the noose became.

Just then, Peter saw the hunters come striding out of the woods on the trail of the greedy wolf, their double-barrelled shotguns gleaming in the sunlight, poised and ready. "*Stop shooting!*" Peter shouted, but the hunters couldn't hear him! Again, he shouted: "*Stop! Put away your guns. Birdie and I have caught the wolf.*"

And then the victory parade! Peter at the head,
followed by the hunters leading the wolf.
And at the rear of the column, Pussy and
Grandfather, still puffing on his pipe,
shaking his head quizzically.
He thought to himself: "Well, *if Peter hadn't*
caught the wolf, huh? – what then?" But he
decided to stay silent. Pussy said nothing.
Above flew Birdie. She was quite pleased
with herself. "*Just look what myself and Peter*
have caught!" she chirped.

And if you listen, you just might hear that dumb duck quacking away inside the belly of the wolf.

You see, in his hungry attack, the wolf had swallowed her alive.

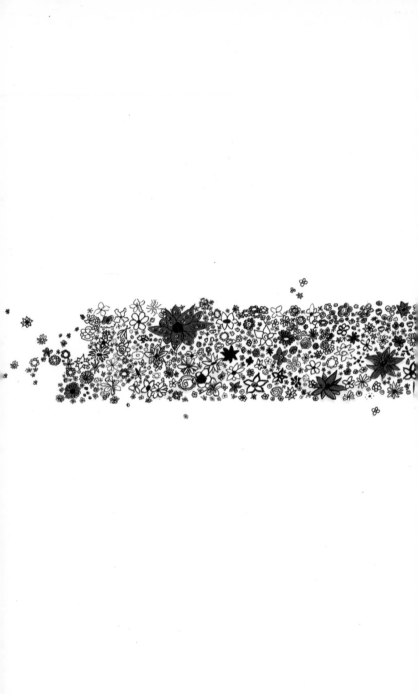

IN AID OF HOSPICE CARE

The *Peter & The Wolf* project was developed by a small team of voluntary supporters of the Irish Hospice Foundation, a not-for-profit organisation dedicated to supporting the development of hospice care. Hospice care is about helping people to live life fully to the end. It is about respect for human life and helping people to face death with dignity by making available the care and support they and their families need.

Peter & The Wolf has been brought to life by the talents of Gavin Friday, Maurice Seezer, the Friday-Seezer Ensemble, Bono and Ciarán ÓGaora. Funds raised by this project will be administered by the foundation to benefit hospice care internationally.

www.peterwolf.org

BONO

Bono is the lead singer of the Irish rock group U2. U2 released its first record in April 1980, and have since sold over 100 million albums worldwide.

Since 1998, Bono has been an active supporter of the international *Jubilee 2000 Drop the Debt* campaign, which campaigned for the debt cancellation of the world's poorest countries. He has used his fame to get the media to pay attention to debt, poverty and AIDS in Africa, and to get access to the world's most powerful politicians.

Bono, along with *Live Aid's* Sir Bob Geldof, has set up a network called DATA (*Debt, AIDS, Trade in Africa*), which targets rich governments to increase resources and improve their policies towards African countries.

Bono lives in Dublin, Ireland, with his wife and four children. Eve and Jordan, Bono's daughters, painted many of the flowers in the *Peter & The Wolf* illustrations.

GAVIN FRIDAY

Gavin Friday was born in Dublin in October 1959. He survived a Christian Brothers education to become a singer, composer and painter. He was the founder member of the legendary avant-garde punk group, The Virgin Prunes. Since 1985 he has composed and performed with his longtime musical partner Maurice Seezer.

FRIDAY-SEEZER albums include *Each Man Kills the Thing He Loves*, *Adam 'n' Eve* and *Shag Tobacco*. Film Scores include *In the Name of the Father*, *The Boxer* and *Disco Pigs*. Stage shows include the Kurt Weill extravaganza, *Ich Liebe Dich*. Forthcoming releases include the score to Jim Sheridan's *In America*.

www.gavinfriday.com

MAURICE SEEZER

Maurice Seezer was born in Dublin in September 1960. He studied piano, cello and harmony at the Royal Academy of Music and didn't like punk. He went to Trinity College, Dublin, to study the Bible, played piano in bars and conducted the College Singers until he met Gavin through a mutual friend.

THE ENSEMBLE

Gavin Friday
Narration

Maurice Seezer
Accordion, piano

Renaud Pion
Bass clarinet

Michael Blair
Drums percussion, tuned percussion

Des Moore
Banjo, mandolin, guitar

Gareth Hughes
Bass

Julia Palmer
Cello

Catriona Ryan
Piccolo, flute

Paddy Boland
The wolf

CREDITS

MUSIC
Produced and arranged by
Gavin Friday and Maurice Seezer
Orchestratation adapted for Ensemble by
Maurice Seezer
Recorded and mixed by Andrew Boland,
Windmill Lane Recording Studios, Dublin
Pro tools – Andrew Boland
Pre-production – The 'Horse' Studio, Dublin
Post-production – Corrig Studios, Dublin
Copyist – Brian and John Byrne
Mastered by Nick Webb,
Abbey Road Studios, London
Friday-Seezer legal and business affairs –
Gaby Smith & Co.
Catriona Ryan has appeared with kind
permission of the RTÉ Authority
Copyright of Friday-Seezer arrangement –
Boosey & Hawkes

VISUALS
Illustrations – Bono, Jordan & Eve

Design and art direction – Ciarán ÓGaora

Enhanced CD & website – Digital:CC
Photography – Perry Ogden, Neil Gavin
Film – Dreamchaser Productions

***

Very special thanks to
Gavin, Maurice, Bono, Jordan and Eve

www.peterwolf.org

Project Team
Marie Donnelly
(Project Director)
Aisling Carr
Sebastian Clayton
Tim Collins
Aileen Corkery
Barry Devlin
Kathy Gilfillan
Ciarán ÓGaora
Perry Ogden
Eileen Pearson
Robert Power
Pete Reddy

Special Thanks
Andrew Boland
James Hickey
Paul McGuinness
Sheila Roche
Ed Victor

Thanks
All at Bloomsbury
Sharon Blankson
Clare Boland
Candida Bottaci
Mary Bruton
Anne-Marie Butler
Gillian Buckley
Guggi
Ciarán Cahill
Paul Cairo
Dermot Chichester
All at Christie's,
Dublin, London,
Los Angeles
& New York

Bob Collins
Emer Connolly
James Cooke
Sarah Dempsey
Designworks.ie
Digital:CC
Jed Donnelly
Joe Donnelly
Dublin City Council
Joe Edwards
Tana Edwards
Caroline Erskine
Mary Furlong
Barbara Galavan
Susan Hunter
All at the Irish
Hospice Foundation
JAB
Keryn Kaplan
Ann-Louise Kelly
Maurice Linnane
Gerry MacArthur
Jean Manahan
Kate Miller

Brian Moore
Régine Moylett
Michael O'Doherty
The Office of Public
Works, Dublin
Robbie O'Halloran
Ned O'Hanlon
Maria Pizzuti
All at Principle
Management
All at the Royal
Hibernian Academy,
Dublin
Christine Ryall
Sarah Sherry
Bill Shipsey
Bernard Williams